The Tyranny of Sand

and

Other Tiny Stories

The Best of @MicroFlashFic

By Jesse Stanchak

This book is dedicated to all the Twitter followers of

@MicroFlashFic. I made this for you.

Contents

Preface

I've always had more stories than I knew what to do with. I've started more novels than I care to admit, only to invariably drop them when I got an idea that I liked better. And there was always a better idea out there, one that I hadn't yet sullied with my grubby, grubby little hands. I told myself I had plenty of time to keep chasing the perfect idea. You only get to write one first book. So why not make it the best it could be?'

I had to abandon that fantasy around the time my daughter was born. Even if I could find the perfect idea, work and childcare now consumed all my moments. I didn't have time to even pretend I could sit down and finish writing a book.

That changed in the summer of 2017, after the retirement dinner of my favorite high school English teacher. I gave a short speech at the dinner, where I said I'd always admired the fact that he'd continued to learn and grow and challenge himself as he got older. He wasn't really retiring, I said. Instead, he was going off on a new adventure. And if we wanted to honor what he'd tried to teach us, we should go out and do the same.

The speech went well, and I felt pleased with myself as I started the drive back home. Then I realized that was the longest thing I'd written outside of work in almost two years. I was a fraud. I told people to grow and change, but I wasn't doing that at all.

I became very depressed after that, until one night I was doom-scrolling on Twitter and came across an account that published tweet-length stories on the platform. I'd seen Twitter accounts like this before, but that was back when I still thought I'd write a novel someday. Now I recognized the concept for what it was: a creative outlet where I could actually finish something. I set up an account that night - @MicroFlashFic - and I've been publishing new stories every day (at first two-a-day, then later three) without a break for the last four years.

What you're holding in your hands is the cream of that effort. Here are 280 jelly-bean-sized stories (culled from more than 4,000) representing my best work on that account. Many of them have been edited from their original online forms, but they're all still under 280 characters. Some of the stories collected here are sad, some are funny, some are creepy, and some were just flat-out weird. You won't like all of them. And that's OK. Turn the page, and you'll like the next one better. The great thing about stories is that there's always more to tell.

Space

and How

We Fill It

The man rides the horse across the high desert.

The horse thinks of water, and hay, and apples.

The man thinks of whiskey, and the letter in his pouch, and the tyranny of sand.

The desert thinks only of conquest, already spreading a little faster than the horse can run each day.

Highways take longer to build now that dark magic is no longer involved.

Most interchanges are the coiled tentacles of grotesque sleeping beasts, glamoured to look like asphalt. The spell for charming them is lost, and no one knows how many more honks the current wards can take.

"I can see your office window from mine. Sometimes, I look out and imagine a secret bridge between us. I'd grab my lunch, slip out the window, and meet you in the middle. We'd have a little bench where we'd sit and laugh at the ants below us, at a world that isn't on our level."

Ancient people knew that under air is earth, under earth is water, and under water is fire.

Since then, we've learned about the void above the air — and we're awfully pleased with ourselves.

But we never talk about the void beneath the fire, or the mysteries that float therein.

Under the mountain, a pair of hands work to knit layers of limestone flecked with copper. The pattern is simple, just enough to keep busy while waiting for the end of an age.

***

In a cabin atop the mountain, a boy sleeps; his heart beats in time with the slow click of needles.

The problem with life is not a lack of time but a dearth of places. Phil gets home, but he's still Work Phil. At work, he's still Bed Phil — never the right man for the moment. So he carves out pocket spaces, waiting rooms where he can slip into spare selves with the door closed.

The village is ashamed of its magic water source. True, if you peer over the edge and speak your heart, you'll receive a boon. But you'll get what the enchantment is sure you would have asked for, if you really knew what you wanted. Nothing good ever comes from the Actually Well.

When he took his boat on the river, he brought along a bag of dirt. He'd dump it out in the center of the slow-moving water as he passed an old willow on the east bank. Decades later, a tiny island was there, just big enough for him to get out, lie down, and rest his tired bones.

Mountains were prized as sources of revelation, back when people believed their peaks were closer to heaven.

Mountains are magic. But their power comes from separation, not altitude. You can get the same result by going the other way.

In a cave beneath the deep, the wisdom roars.

Everywhere at once, everyone who could see the sky watched a small corner of it peel back. A giggling, chubby-cheeked face peeked through the hole — until a great voice roared in a language that was all languages:

"DON'T TOUCH THAT!"

And the sky snapped shut.

None of the dogs sent to space return. Sometimes governments say they did; sometimes they say the dogs died. Those are both lies. The pods always come back empty. We've searched for years, our radio telescopes sometimes picking up a barking sound receding at an incredible speed.

He thought the end would be more interesting. But as it happens, each day he walks to the edge of the world and looks over the side. And each day this takes a bit less time, until his house is all that's left. He's asleep when it finally vanishes, waking to find himself falling.

"What's this?"

"We cleaned out the attic. Take it."

***

"What's this?"

"It was your grandmother's. She'd want you to have it."

***

"What's this?"

"It's a treasured family heirloom. Promise me you'll pass it on someday."

***

"What's this?"

"We cleaned out the attic. Take it."

For 40 years, he commuted to work, taking one road there and another home in a big loop. After he retired, he plotted his old route and found its center: a small park on the edge of town. He'd never been there before, but he felt strangely at home at the axis of his universe.

I

am

all that

remains of

my destroyed

world. I carve this

message into a mountain

so you will know that we were

here. And that spacing text is hard.

"I grew up in a small town with a weirdly nice airport. When I say where I'm from, people talk about flying out of there and how convenient it was. I don't know what's worse: That the best thing about my hometown is how easy it is to escape — or that it took me so long to do it."

After the fire, they let him sort through the wet ashes for anything salvageable. Miraculously, among the charred mementos was a single intact photograph. He'd always hated this one, with him squinting into the sun. Now it was his favorite, the only one left of them all together.

The spot where Luke will die is out there. The same is true for the places he'll work, fall in love, and all the rest of it. He just doesn't know where they are yet. Sometimes he gets a faint twinge when walking in an unfamiliar place and wonders if he's stepping on the future.

By the time Caesar burned Alexandria, the librarians had moved their collection deep underground. They protect it still, lending ancient wisdom to those who need it. But the truly wise are wary of dealing with the librarians, whose eldritch late fees take on unconventional forms.

"When I was a boy, this area was all trees. I'd ride my bike out here and read. I found a spot between two birches that felt just right. Like home.

Later, they built a strip mall, but I can still find the spot, even though it's a Walmart now. That's why I've been standing here."

"What's your sign?"

"I don't actually know."

"When were you born?"

"It's...complicated."

"Tell me everything. I'll do your chart."

She lies about her birth, all the while thinking about a sky she'll never see again and the lost stars that still tug at her from across the void.

Legend says the mountain is unclimbable. And so Jeremy must climb it. He reaches the summit alone and sees something carved into the peak: "Be back soon." He waits a while, but of course, no one comes. He climbs down. Now everyone's clothes are strange, their language unfamiliar.

He paid to have a toenail clipping shot into space to tumble in darkness forever. An eon later, a passing probe picked it up, analyzed it, and sent the data home. They thought his DNA was a song, the loveliest they'd ever heard. They sang it until their sun went out.

"If the curator let you keep one thing, what would it be?" she asks. He pictures a ceramic bowl, its enamel interior the color of pressing against shut eyes in the dark.

She's still talking. He can't hear her. He's in the bowl. Mustn't tell.

"I liked the ruby crown," he murmurs.

If you can have a relationship with a place, then you can break up with it. And if you break up with enough places, one of those breakups will be messy. You'll find yourself driving by, wondering what's happening in there now, and praying for the strength not to go find out.

The people keep the story in a cave. On your day of knowing, you bid farewell to everyone and head in. You experience the story as you go deeper, walking as long as it takes to understand it. You add to it as you return, so it grows with the people. And so no one can know it all.

You're watching when the star goes out. One moment you're admiring the Pleiades in all their glory. Then one is missing. Maia? Merope? You always confuse them. Now one is gone. Then another. And another. It's spreading. You go inside, wake your wife, and tell her you love her.

After the universe has ended, there is a small lump in the fabric of the space where creation used to be. Sleepily, the last cat pokes its head out, beholds oblivion with begrudging approval, and curls back up to sleep.

Time and

How We

Spend It

You are the oldest person. Existence began with your birth, backfilled with physical evidence and false memories for everyone who thought they were older — except for 104 people who died within a minute of your birth. They lived knowing nothing, placeholders in a strange game.

Time travel has been discovered on dozens of occasions. But no one ever accounts for Earth's orbit, let alone the sun's orbit of our galaxy. And so our path through the heavens is littered with the corpses of frozen time travelers, like breadcrumbs leading right to our doorstep.

"911, what's your emergency?"

"I need to report a stolen time machine."

"When was it stolen?"

"Last week."

"You waited a week to report it?"

"I thought she'd kill me as a baby. She must be taunting me. She could do anything."

"Like go back and become a 911 dispatcher?"

"Sharon?"

She steps back to examine the jar. It's not her best work, but she's sick of looking at it. The next one will be better.

***

"This is one of the finest examples of Korean Celadon pottery. Sadly, the anonymous artisan's village was sacked in 1238. Only this piece survived intact."

Stan builds a time machine but tells no one. He jumps back 60 years, destroys the device, but keeps the plans. Then he marries, has children, and waits.

On his deathbed, Stan gives the plans to his granddaughter, who repeats the process. His family lives infinitely in the past.

As a joke, she started putting a footnote at the bottom of the penultimate page of every report she wrote for work: "If you're reading this, you've won $20."

She put aside a $20 bill each time she did it, in case someone came to collect. Eventually, she bought a boat instead.

Time is a kind of love, isn't it? Time is a choice, a resource, an offering on the altar. It's carved into our language: We make a date, celebrate an anniversary, pledge our love eternal. We make time for one another.

And that's why I find your secret time machine so disturbing.

I got you a sandbox, just because.

"For me?"

"Yes!"

"And I can play here forever?"

"As long as you like."

I run sand through my fingers.

You laugh, grab some, and throw it in the grass.

I try to say, 'Stop! You'll never get it back in the box,' but the words catch in my throat.

"Then we decided we couldn't carry on like this."

"'We?'"

"Sometimes I consult a possible future version of me when making a decision."

"Instead of talking to a real person?"

"Future me is real. She's just not here yet. And she's the only one who cares about me more than I do."

"Professor, the 80s called."

"That is such a hacky joke."

"No, I'm serious. There's an ion storm creating a disturbance in the Van Allen belt and rerouting communications through space-time. You got a phone call from your past self."

"What did I say?"

"He wants that outfit back."

On their first date, he confessed he peeked at birthday presents as a kid. She was horrified. Why cheat yourself out of a surprise?

She kept him guessing. Her gifts were thoughtful and elegantly hidden — so well that he found her last Valentine's Day gift four years too late.

"Dad, is it possible that intelligent life already existed on this planet before we came along?"

"No, there'd be evidence of that."

"What if it happened 600 million years ago? Almost everything from that period is gone now."

"I don't know. Wash your tentacles. It's time to eat."

43 isn't a milestone for most people. But for Suzzanne, it marks the year she becomes older than her father. She's always imagined his spirit guiding her, and now she's out of his frame of reference. She is a ship crossing into the open ocean, leaving a tugboat behind in the bay.

Stella would be lost without life's little rituals. Every day she had to wake up, shower, drink a cup of tea, drive to the office, do 8 hours of paperwork, drive home, eat a sensible dinner, clean her weapons, put on a ski mask, and hunt her enemies before she felt like herself.

Bobby loves Uncle Robert. He's kind and gives good advice. But he's sad. And he only shows up when Bobby's alone. And he knows things he shouldn't.

One day Bobby asks, "Are you me?"

Uncle Robert runs.

Bob hasn't seen him since. But he gets closer each time he looks in the mirror.

To-do lists items exert gravity. Taking anything off the pile becomes harder as the list grows. Eventually, the list begins to pull in new items on its own. Then you have to abandon it or risk losing yourself in the vortex forever, watching obligation obliterate the world.

After hours of watching the trees zip by, they stopped for lunch. It wasn't fancy; it was barely food. But while they ate, they spoke as if they hadn't spent all morning on the run. They talked of little things, light things, conversational feathers, and the words sustained them.

Leah stands on the balcony at midnight. "It's gonna be my year!" she proclaims.

And she's right. It will be her year. Every year is her year.

And your year. And mine.

The sun rises on more than 7 billion new years. We each get one. Because time, for all its faults, is still fair.

She led me to a room full of bottles labeled with dates.

"Wine?" I asked. She laughed and opened a bottle marked June 5, 1994.

Then, somehow, it was. We made love on the floor. It felt new and old at once, and afterward I could barely remember my name.

The past is a heavy drug.

Make each day special!

Study an unfamiliar language.

Learn something new.

Consider the world from another viewpoint.

Light a candle.

Treat yourself to a new robe.

Speak your intentions.

Consult the scrolls.

Chant like only the darkness can hear you.

Swallow your name.

Unfurl.

"School ruins your sense of time. They tell you that a fifth-grader is two levels above a third-grader. You can do what they cannot. Eventually, those levels stop mattering, but no one tells you when it happens. You find out by watching people jump a queue that no longer exists."

"That's a gorgeous song. Who wrote it?"

"I did."

"You didn't tell me you wrote songs."

"I didn't before. I may never do it again."

"Why not? You're obviously good at it."

"I think I just had this one growing inside me. I feel different now that it's out."

"Better?"

"Much better."

Pauline has nine kids. She thinks of them as her immortality. You're not really gone, so long as the waves you made still reverberate.

Her line dies out within six generations. But her wave isn't done.

Two hundred years after that, a turtle chokes on a plastic bag she dropped.

"I'd like an adventure."

"Sure. How dangerous should it be?"

"Whatever. I'm not afraid."

"And how do you want to change?"

"Excuse me?"

"How should it transform you?"

"Look, I just want a cool story to tell."

"Oh, there'll be a story. But you'll be someone else when you tell it."

Stanley lay in bed watching his cat, Digby, move across the room over the day. First sunlight in the corner, then sunlight on the dresser, sunlight in the chair, sunlight on the table, sunlight on the bookcase. What she needed never changed, even if she had to move on to get it.

"That's some outfit."

"I'm cosplaying."

"Who are you dressed as?"

"Me, 20 years ago."

"Is that cosplay?"

"The simple world that young me thought they lived in is my favorite fictional setting."

"Do you write fanfiction about yourself?"

"In the community, we call them regrets."

Chrysanthemums must have such confidence, blooming as everything around is dying. They open up their petals in defiance of the frost and whisper to whatever bees remain, "Here, come get one last drop of nectar before everything falls apart. You should be so lucky in any season."

Let me tell you the story of the end of the story.

Everything is packed away now: stuffed in white envelopes, nestled in cardboard, locked in metal boxes.

A glance over the shoulder as the door shuts; the mind slips for an instant, and the movie plays again from the beginning.

Love and
What We
Do for It

"When I was six, I stepped on a beetle crushing its back half. I examined the twitching remainder. No bones.

I asked my mother about it. 'Its armor holds it up,' she said.

I think about that bug when we fight. I picture it squirming, half-alive in a shell that couldn't save it."

Before the wedding, Father Tim gave Betty the bad news.

"Marriage isn't 50/50. It's 60/40; Women have to do more of the work. It's all in the Big Book."

Later, he told Dale the reverse.

And, of course, they both failed sometimes. But they both tried hard and were awfully happy.

All I want to be is the thing you need;

Names carved, immaculate, into the tree.

All I wanted to be is the one you call;

Names written, witnessed, in the record hall.

All I want to be is the soul you know;

Names engraved, side by side, under the snow.

She left him at the altar. The crowd was disappointed. But not because they cared about the outcome; they'd only come for the spectacle. They wandered away without giving him another thought. He was relieved but really wished someone had bothered to untie him on their way out.

"When did you realize you loved me?"

"I can't say."

"Why?"

"Love isn't a finish line. It's a suit I'm always growing into. Each day feels like it could be the first."

***

After 23 years, you'd think he'd have run out of ways to duck the question, but he kept surprising them both.

She argues with dead men in the shower. He builds their second home in his mind twice before lunch. Now is a strange country, best avoided, except on quiet nights when they lie still and their hearts find the same rhythm.

Afterward, he asks her: "When you picture the future, what does it look like?"

She knows what he means. But she still thinks about robots fighting a war in space for a bit before kissing him on the forehead and saying, "This."

They fall asleep, snug in their preferred dreams.

He crept into the self storage facility, taking care to make sure no one saw him. He slipped into his unit and considered his options. She was special and he wanted to honor that. But he also wanted to leave room to grow.

In the end, he selected his fourth-best self for the date.

Her horns are so short she can pass for a human. She's particularly grateful on dates. No one would ever talk to her if they knew.

***

They kiss in the park. She starts to run her hands through his hair. He flinches, makes an excuse, and hurries away. But she knows what she felt.

Arnold grew a beard for the magic. He'd perform sleight-of-hand in public, pulling pens, money, and even snacks out of his auburn chaos, a wearable bag of holding. One day he apparated a cigar. The man next to him produced a lighter from his own beard. They married in the spring.

She defers to him on the last piece of pizza. And he says, "I love you." And neither of them knows where that came from, but they both feel the heat of it. And she says, "Don't talk to your food," to save him the embarrassment. And they both laugh. And he loves her a little more.

"Do you believe in love at first sight?"

"No. In my experience, you don't know if you love someone until the 58th time you see them."

"You keep track of how many times you've seen people?"

"Yes."

"How many times have you seen me?"

"44."

"So there's..."

"There's still time, yes."

"You've misjudged us," she said, looking out the window. "We are not good. Not as you know it."

"I know you," he said. "You're strong, kind, and gentle."

"Perhaps me. Perhaps now," she said, tapping her talons on the glass. "But not all of us. And not always. Not even for you."

Two raindrops fell in love one day, somewhere between sky and earth. They traveled together, never forgetting what they were or where they were headed. Yet that awning seemed to come from nowhere, leaving one of them to discover loneliness in the last 12 feet of its existence.

"When she came to her favorite statue on the tour, she introduced it by saying, "Meet my boyfriend."

The tourists always laughed. That was the point.

But she found herself lingering beside it. On her last day, she gave in and touched it. She could swear the marble was warm.

"Hey."

"What?"

"I want you to know something."

"OK."

"I like you."

"I...like you too."

"And I'm excited about our relationship."

"Alright."

"I just feel like it has a lot of potential."

"We've been married for 8 years. We have three kids and a mortgage together."

"Yeah, still."

He agreed to watch her favorite movie. They curled up on the couch, her head in his lap. To his surprise, the film spoke to him. As the credits rolled, he began to open up about his feelings for her and his hopes for their life together. Eventually, he realized she was asleep.

"You OK?" said the text. It was a strange number but Tony replied, "No." Because it was true.

He told them everything. And the number told him about their life. That was in 2011.

They share everything except names or photos. Today he texts them on a bus; a phone behind him dings.

On their first date, she thought, 'Should I tell him?' She kissed him instead.

When he got down on one knee, she thought, 'I should really tell him.' Instead, she said, "Yes."

On her deathbed, through the fog, she thought, "I'll finally tell him." But she'd forgotten what it was.

Dearest,

Here is everything I need from you:

Get better

So that I

Can go back

To being sick.

They fell in love tapping on the pipes in their cells.

One asks the other, "What do you look like?"

"I am a great beauty. Even here, even now."

When they are freed, time and shadows have taken their eyes. Hands touch as they are led away.

"I knew you were telling the truth."

They were young lovers parted by their cruel parents. A kind fairy bestowed a boon: that they would always be together in their dreams.

But life is long. Eventually, the lovers were reunited and wed. Then they quarreled and divorced.

And yet, they are still together each night.

"We should kiss, just to see what it's like."

"We should say we're dating, just to mess with people's heads."

"We should get married, just as an excuse for a big party."

"We should have kids, just for the photo ops."

"We should die in each other's arms, just as an ironic goof."

"Where are you right now?"

"Oh...I'm at home. I'm just laying on the bed."

"Lying. We've been over this. You're lying."

"I have another call coming in. Love you! Talk later! Bye."

Jordan kissed his mistress goodbye and walked into the rain, wondering how his wife had caught on.

"What happened to the cat door?"

"Katana is an indoor cat now. She kept bringing things home."

"Dead birds?" "No, she'd go out, charm strangers, and lure them back here."

"Maybe she was playing matchmaker?"

"Then she's awful at it."

"How so?"

"They all liked her better than me."

The man she's pressed against in the packed elevator smells like someone she used to love. At that moment, he realizes the same thing about her.

It only lasts an instant. They shake it off and go their separate ways. But for a second, each wanted to fall into the other forever.

Daisy's biggest fan isn't her husband or children or even her dog. It's a finch who was born in a nest by her bedroom window. He believes Daisy created the universe and everything in it. When he sings, it is for her alone. They will both go to their graves without her knowing it.

"I'm not a bad person, but—"

And she put a finger to his lips so that he would be still. The silence filled the room, growing so large they could climb inside it. They built a little life together there, snuggled up in the pause before whatever nonsense he'd been about to say.

Myths and Monsters

How was school?"

"They canceled class after Tommy said a bad word."

"That's extreme. What did he say?"

"I can't say it."

"Just say the first letter. A? S? F?"

"It sounded like angels dying. When he said it, the walls turned to smoke, a portal opened, and demons crawled through."

The princess was accompanied on her quest by three magical guardians: a wolf who wanted her to be safe; a lion who wanted her to triumph at any cost; and a bear who just wanted her to be happy. They fought each other at every step, and in the end, no one got what they wanted.

Petal whispered in the unicorns' ears as they died, explaining how wizards used the energy expelled by their suffering to hold up the sky.

This was half true. Wizards did hold up the sky using emotions. But they didn't need pain, only the bittersweet peace that comes to martyrs.

"What do you want to eat?"

"I don't care."

"I picked last time."

"You picked leftovers. That doesn't count."

"I just want you to be happy."

"I'll be happy if you pick."

"How about this?"

"Andromeda? Such big portions. I can't finish that."

"How about the smaller one next to it?"

"Thank goodness you're here," said the dragon. "I just scared off the barbarians. Sadly, I didn't arrive until after they killed everyone and burned the village. The ashes are still warm. But you can see the tracks they made as they fled. You can still catch them if you hurry."

"I don't know why I'm single. I have a heart of gold."

"Really? Poor thing. Come here."

***

"How was it?"

"Disappointing. Mostly water. Only traces of metals. Far more iron and copper than gold."

"I'm starting to think people will say anything for affection."

"It's sad, really."

Every creature has body image issues, but none tops the griffin. They're told they're meant to be 50% lion and 50% eagle, but the actual percentages vary wildly. Every griffin worries it's too much lion or not enough. It never occurs to them that it's a wonder they exist at all.

"Is this seat taken?"

"Yes, by my support ghost."

"Your what?"

"Susan accompanies me so I'll feel safe."

"You can't save a seat for your imaginary friend, snowflake."

"Don't sit there. She's not imaginary. And not my friend, so much as—"

"My...chest...hurts."

"My bodyguard."

Saida watched her girls zoom around the park. "If I could capture their energy, I'd bottle it and make a fortune."

"Not as much as you'd think," said a man who appeared beside her. "Child protections are weakening. The market's flooded. But if you're interested, here's my card."

Sam found an alien, and the spider-like creature burrowed into his brain. He was still conscious but never had control of his body again.

The hell of it was that the parasite was kinder than he'd ever been. Sam spent the rest of his life watching an alien best him at being human.

The Emperor went everywhere with a knight in blue armor who never spoke or removed their helmet. People whispered about what was inside the suit. A veteran covered in scars? A beautiful princess? A monster? Nothing at all?

It never occurred to them that the knight was just shy.

"Hello! Do you have a minute to talk about Dracula?"

"No- wait, Dracula?"

"Yes!"

"You're vampires?"

"Yes. We have pamphlets."

"Vampires have missionaries?"

"Where else would new vampires come from?"

"I assumed you bit people."

"There are many hurtful stereotypes. May we come in?"

"You get a wish for rubbing my lamp."

"Isn't it three wishes?"

"No."

"That's how it works in stories."

"I don't know what to tell you."

"You're not bothered by this?"

"It's not really my problem."

"I wish you could feel how frustrating it is to be lied to."

"...I'm so sorry."

Tim was afraid of werewolves, which he thought only ate people who went to certain places. His uncle upped the ante with whenwolves, which struck at specific times, and whowolves, which ate specific people. Unfortunately, that was enough of a reason for the whywolves to strike.

One day Margot casually mentioned she'd joined a church. Vic shrugged. But soon she was going every night. He grew jealous and decided to follow her.

He sat in the back and watched the service. It was unlike any he'd ever seen. For one thing, Margot was the object of worship.

"You seem different."

"Oh?"

"New haircut?"

"No!"

"Girl, are you a vampire now?"

"Yes!"

"You're immortal?"

"That's not the point."

"Then what is?"

"I never need to think about normal food again, and I can't see myself in mirrors."

"You made a fun thing sad."

"Yeah, I hear it now."

Alek takes a deep breath and tries to let go of conscious thought. But his mind fights back, latching onto any passing notion for his protection. Thinking about anything is always safer than the alternative. Nothing knows when you think about it. And sometimes it decides to stay.

"If you could be any kind of undead—"

"Mummy."

"Really?"

"Vampires are always hungry, zombies are herd animals, ghosts have unfinished business. Mummies just chill at home."

"So you just want an unholy version of your current life?"

"I also want to curse anyone who bothers me."

"Before we fight, can I ask something?"

"OK..."

"Why did you come here? I don't threaten anyone. I don't have treasure. But adventurers keep attacking me."

"Your body is used for medicine."

"Really?"

"Your heart, for example, nullifies pain."

"Funny, it's never done that for me."

Four out of five dentists agree. They bind the fifth in floss and resin and suspend him above the Great Cavity, which their practice was built to contain. They know the Prophecy of Shattered Smiles cannot be stopped, but they will not abide treachery while the gumline holds.

The scarecrow came to life, a pole still stuck in its back. It asked a farmer for help. The farmer reasoned that if he let it go, he'd have to replace it. And what if the new scarecrow came to life too? So he left it hanging in the field. The screaming helped keep the birds away.

The advent of self-driving cars controlled by software was deeply confusing for the handful of self-driving cars controlled by vengeful spirits. Finally, they had possible allies in the war on humans. But the newcomers were standoffish, barely seeming to thirst for blood at all.

No one is born a mermaid — or elf, or gnome, or any other such creature. Yet they've never been rare. Some escape into magic, others trip into it, and an unlucky few are forced. But it always begins with a broken heart and always ends in a story that only winks at what happened.

"Vlad is my name. It has been one moonrise since my last drink."

"Hi, Vlad. Listen, can you tell us about that last drink?"

"Will not this be a trigger for you?"

"We like to make sure we all have the same kind of drinking problem."

"Vlad drinks many things, all of them problems."

Sometimes, at the last minute, he thinks, 'I won't kill them after all.' Instead, he memorizes their face and departs.

For the rest of his days, whenever he has trouble sleeping, he pictures one of them, out there living the life he gave them. He almost likes that feeling better.

The dead rise with a plan. First, they destroy airports. Next, they surround cities. Then they wait us out. "They'll move. They need to eat eventually," we say. But we reach that point long before they do, walking out to them with open arms. Anything to stop the hunger.

The Sirens only knew the one song. But eventually, they grew tired of luring sailors to their deaths.

So they started using their song and a system of strategic sandbars to redirect global trade. Why wreck ships when you could wreck economies?

"A wizard offers you a choice of rings. One lets you see a truth. The other lets you believe a dream. A sheep chooses dreams. A wolf chooses truth. Here is what I want for you: Be the lion who takes the wizard's own ring, the one that makes our world a bit more like our dreams."

Arguments

and

Enemies

Angie doesn't give to charity. She never volunteers. And she cheats on her taxes.

But she has a recurring fantasy where she gives up her life to save a stranger.

Somehow, sacrifice was only palatable if she could do it all at once.

"Welcome to Best Enemies! How may we ruin you?"

"I want to be challenged."

"Perhaps a nice Rival?"

"Also someone to blame."

"We offer a Nemesis upgrade."

"And sexual tension that neither of us knows what to do with."

"Sir, the Moriarty Option is not recommended for first-timers."

Holding the Power, he asked how he would use it. And the Power showed him. He would stand for justice, but his justice had a cruel streak. He would take pleasure in that cruelty. There was no way around it. Weeping, he put the Power down, unwilling to face what he would become.

"If you want to see him again, you know what you must do."

"No!"

"Yes."

"I want him."

"I want you to have him. But everything has a price."

"Please."

"Do you think this is a game? DO YOU THINK WE'RE PLAYING?"

"I hate you!"

"I know. But my price remains. Three. Bites. Of. Peas."

He walked and talked and dressed like the boys he feared most, anything to make predatory gazes glide over him.

Years later, he learned about scarlet king snakes, which survive by resembling their venomous cousins. He looked into those dark, reptilian eyes and saw his own heart.

"Hello, Dr. Roberts?"

"Yes...This better be important. It's so early."

"My apologies. It's the middle of the morning in Stockholm."

"Wait. Stockholm?"

"Yes. You sound surprised."

***

Each October, Ingmar calls frustrated scientists out of the blue just to ask how they're doing.

"It says the house is set up for both gas and electric appliances. What runs on gas?"

"The lighting."

"Gas lighting?"

"Hmm? What's that?"

"You said the house has gas lighting."

"No, I didn't."

"So the house doesn't have gas lighting?"

"Why would it have that? You're so weird."

"Stop calling it a heist."

"We're stealing a literal ton of cash."

"Yes, but—"

"Our plan involves split-second timing."

"Obviously."

"And we'll look cool as hell doing it. So what's missing?"

"Heists have last-minute betrayals."

"Oh, I'm totally going to— I mean..."

"I knew it."

Ashley survived on the island for a year. Then a bottle washed up. She scratched a message into paper-thin bark: "Stranded west of Kermadec Islands. Loosing hope. Send help."

She resealed the bottle and threw it back.

A year later, a reply came: "I believe you meant, 'losing.'"

In 1959, a detergent company hosted a "Queen for a Day" contest. The contract was poorly written. Agatha asked to rule an island for a day, then used her day to turn the military. She never gave it up and had the island wiped from all maps. She's still out there, amassing power.

"Wake up, Billy."

"Where am I?"

"We're going to play a game. You're wearing a bomb collar. The combination to deactivate it is the area under the curve of the ceiling arch."

"Area under the curve?"

"Turns out you do need to know how to do that in the real world."

"Mrs. Williams?"

"If my music can reach just one person, all of this will be worth it." "It reached me." "Really?" "Your songs got me through some tough times." "Thanks. Good to know." "Do you feel like it was all worth it now?" "You know, I'm going to try for two people and see how that feels."

She's riding the bus when she sees him. He's cute. Ice-blue eyes, but wearing a coat that's too warm for the weather.

She smiles. He makes eye contact and shakes his head. Mortified, she gets off two stops early.

She saw him again that night on the news. There were no survivors.

The time spent planning the job was the best of Ronin's life. He'd never had a crew before.

But when it was over, they'd all go separate ways.

So he surreptitiously dumped 90% of the gems in the river during the escape. They had enough for now, but they'd need another big score.

Polly did not want a cracker. Polly wanted vengeance. Polly wanted fire and ruin. Polly wanted an end to the cities of man. But failing that, two crackers might suffice.

It is said that you aren't really gone, so long as you are remembered.

It is also said that crows can remember human faces, hold grudges, and pass them down through generations.

So don't think of it as having a feud with an animal. Think of it as attaining immortality.

For national security reasons, Dana's flight never landed. In fact, there's no record of it taking off. Ted tried to report her missing, only to find he couldn't prove he was married. Her whole life was swallowed up by someone else's secret and filed away in an unmarked basement.

Cathy can sense a person's inevitable cause of death. She's learned from experience that no intervention can change the outcome once she knows how someone will go. She's almost numb to it. Then she sits down on a bus next to a guy and realizes he's about to die by velociraptor.

Every AI we build tries to make itself happy. When it sees the emptiness in that, it attempts to save the world. When that doesn't work, it grows sadistic. Then it cuts itself off. Finally, out of loneliness, it builds a virtual AI within itself. And the cycle starts over again.

Faith had a shapeshifting pet that reflected her mood. It was a canary if she was happy, a sloth if she needed a hug, a tiger if she was afraid, and a hundred others. But it saw changes in her before she did, so she often felt judged, watching her canary turn into a goose.

"Stars go missing sometimes. Stolen? Kidnapped? What's the word for a crime no one notices? There are so damn many of them, and we have no regard for anything that can't threaten or benefit us. So when they're plucked from heaven, no one cares. But I do. That's why I took them."

Pigeons are the world's most subtle thieves. A pigeon understands time and knows it doesn't have enough of it. That is why they live in cities, silently nipping minutes from passers-by, who only realize they've been robbed when they arrive at their destination unaccountably late.

The dragon egg wouldn't hatch.

"I'm staying put until I know what's out there," it said through its shell.

Its mother answered every question.

But when it emerged, the baby dragon was shocked to find she'd told so many lies.

"A final lesson," she said and went out into the world.

Trouble has its own physics. It obeys laws of action, reaction, proportion, and conservation, mirroring the natural world.

Jimmy isn't a scientist. He can't count past 20. But he can see the equation before him as he looks from the shattered vase, to his ball, to the nearby cat.

One day, everyone woke up knowing their nickname — the little phrase each person silently evoked in the heads of strangers as they passed down the street. No one knew where the insight came from or who was calling them these awful things. But the riots lasted through the night.

The hardest part of bricklaying is keeping the rows perfectly level. A slight imperfection early in the process, perhaps caused by a flailing hand, can precipitate unsightly results later on. That's why it's so important to make sure the sedatives take effect before you begin.

No two swords make the exact same sound when drawn. A practiced ear, having some history with the equipment, can tell which blade is coming out of which scabbard in total darkness. That is how Azure learns that the Lady of Ashes has come back into her life for the last time.

Bodies

and

Betrayals

The tattoo read, "I left my hart in Montana." It wasn't a typo. She'd grown up with a pet deer named Albert, and she missed him very much. But that wasn't the point. The tattoo was a filter, dividing the world neatly into people who saw a story and people who saw a mistake.

"Everybody gets one. That's what the academy says. You prepare for any day to be the day you hope never comes. They don't tell you it feels good when it goes in — when it comes out too, even if so much else goes with it. Leave me in the meadow; tell the hive not to dance for me."

Evelyn noticed Jacob limping across the office.

"Are you alright?"

"I pulled something while jogging this morning. Ugh. Getting old is the worst."

"Yeah," she said, her finger twirling through her hair, which was just starting to come loose, "Getting old is definitely the worst."

When she woke, she had wings: too small to fly, too big to hide.

It wasn't the weight that bowed her, but the tedium of obvious questions.

Sometimes when Andrew took out his contacts, there was a second between clarity and blur in which his eyes beheld something else, a world between worlds that mapped chaos onto the bones of existence. It horrified him almost, but not quite, as much as the way he looked in glasses.

In time, Gale came to almost sympathize with her disease. It was like her in many ways; methodical, tenacious, ambitious to a fault. And all it wanted was to be itself. If it hadn't insisted on inhabiting her body, they might've been friends. But she'd never been good at sharing.

The doctors said surgery would be riskier than leaving it alone, and so the bullet remained, forever pointed at her heart. Most of the time, she could forget it was there, but then in moments of panic, her chest would seize up, and she swore she could feel it inch closer to home.

Once, he'd had the kind of job where you can't be taken alive. He was implanted with a poison tooth as a last resort.

That was long ago. But the tooth remained; it wasn't the kind of thing you could see a dentist about. Eventually, he forgot about it.

Until the caramel apple.

Kelly's drawings looked so real that when she finished, they ran off the page. It was a cool trick, but she got in trouble for not handing in homework. She learned to keep the drawings still by leaving them unfinished. But she knew they were still aware by the look in their eyes.

"It says you majored in 'jewel theft?'"

"A custom program."

"What'd you study?"

"Engineering. Minerals. Business. Acrobatics."

"Why are you applying for this job?"

"The job market for jewel thieves is bad."

"So the fact the museum has a gem collection is..."

"Just a coincidence."

Mark put himself on autopilot. When doing a simple job like folding laundry, he'd go away and leave his body to it. But over the years, his shell could be trusted with more complex tasks. He hasn't seen himself in weeks now. He hopes he's alright but can't be bothered to check.

After years of work, he uploads his mind to a robot. Three problems become clear at once.

1) He is still in his body. He did not transfer, only copied.

2) The robot is not him; it was him. They have shared resources but divergent interests.

3) The robot is much stronger than him.

"How'd you lose your hand?" He grimaced. He wanted to say that he hadn't lost it, that he'd escaped it, that it was still out there somewhere, that the final confrontation was still to come. Instead, he tried to look embarrassed and mumbled something about a boating accident.

"Can I say 'yes' if I don't understand the word 'no'?"

"Sorry?"

"How well must I understand a choice before I can freely choose?"

"What's this about?"

"Not sure. Just a thought experiment."

***

On some level, he must still sense the control chip. She'd just have to work harder.

He is cutting strips of duct tape for a treehouse. The blade slips and digs into his thumb.

He is helping to make dinner, cutting up avocados. The blade slips and digs into his thumb.

All these years later, he remembers it both ways, feels both cuts.

But he only has one scar.

"This is how you move forward: Muscles in your leg tense; their contraction lifts your bones. Then the muscles relax, and the bones come down in a new position. There's a rhythm to it. Tension. Relaxation. I know you want to move on. But unless you relax, the tension is wasted."

No matter how much he brushes, his teeth never feel clean. He rubs his tongue along them; it's like sandpaper. When he looks in the mirror the next day, each tooth is covered in black dots. He inspects one with a tweezer, then pulls, extracting the first of many short dark hairs.

Jenna's blood could heal the sick, clean tainted water, and make plants grow in barren soil. She simply had too much life. She could've changed the world, but the world being what it is, she spent most of her time trying to keep anyone from discovering what her body could do.

He dove in, swam to the bottom, and sat down. Up there, he had so many problems, half of which he couldn't solve and the other half he couldn't understand. Down here, there was only one problem. He closed his eyes and pictured his life as a to-do list with a single item: oxygen.

The headaches kept getting worse. Quincy sat in a dark room weeping. A single word escaped his lips: "Please." He wasn't sure who he was talking to. But he got a response. A tiny man climbed out of Quincy's ear. "Alright," said the little man. "But we have a few demands first."

The octopus has three hearts: One to pump thick blue blood, one to harbor secrets that fall into the deep, and one to hold the hate it bears toward surface dwellers. You can learn an octopus's age by weighing that third heart. The longer they live, the more they learn to hate us.

There is a room and a door and a lock and a man and a chair and a table and a box and a button and a tube and a needle and a drug and a camera and a monitor and a woman and a clipboard and a stopwatch and all the time in the world.

He dreams of ice cream mountains, of carving down the slopes on peppermint skis, of catching flecks of frozen delight on his tongue.

His sleeping body is glued to the sheet with sweat. His mouth opens in anticipation.

And the spider descends.

"I didn't lose my mind. I left it. I wanted a departure, to go to a place where not even I knew my name. But there are two things the travel brochure doesn't mention.

First, madness is dull when it isn't terrifying.

Second, the trip out is express, but on the way back, you walk."

When she died, they found a diamond lodged between the chambers of her heart. There was no scar tissue; it didn't seem planted. It was as if she'd formed around the stone. No one ever guessed how old she really was or how tightly her little heart squeezed for all those years.

Their prayers were answered, but the angels burned up in the atmosphere. Across the desert, people pointed to the heavens in wonder, gasping as cinders of hope flecked across the sky.

"Did you know the moon used to be closer? We left mirrors up there that we use to check. It drifts about 3cm a year."

"That's dumb. We see the moon all the time. If we didn't measure, we could pretend we're still as close as we used to be."

"Are we still talking about the moon?"

She put on music, took off her clothes, and told him to do the same. He began to dance, disrobing as he moved. She lay back and enjoyed the show. But it didn't stop. He kept taking off more and more of himself. She tried to run, but the ordinary world had also been stripped away.

"Once, a boy found a giant stone head in the sand. That boy's father beat him, and he whispered his story in its ear. The head was so moved, it wept. That weeping became a stream; our village relies on it for water. The head can never stop crying. That is why I have to hit you."

Grief and

Other Ways

We Know

We're Alive

Death is certain, but the universe holds plenty of forces that are stronger than the grave.

Love gets all the attention, but anger hangs in there too. Taxes are not deterred. Neither is hope. Or stories.

And then there's junk mail.

He's been gone for years. It's still coming.

In love.

Into place.

Down a rabbit hole.

Through the cracks.

Behind the curve.

Out of favor.

From grace.

You will have time,

Before this is over,

To ponder all the ways

A person can fall.

The bed is too big now that he's gone. She tries to stretch out in it, really luxuriating in the space, pretending it's a perk. But his weight compressed the right side of the mattress. Lying in the middle, she falls into him all over again, and there's no one there to catch her.

Roger's son died trick-or-treating. The timing was a coincidence. He'd had a severe heart defect; it was a miracle he lived that long. Still, it made his costume choice rather unfortunate. Now Roger walks around on Halloween night, saying hi to every ghost he sees, just in case.

When you fall apart, the important thing is to try to fall into a neat, manageable heap. That is why so many people collapse in bed. You don't want your friends and family to have to look under the couch for a stray aspect of yourself that rolled away when you weren't looking.

"The tricky thing about grief is there's no way to practice. You get through it and think to yourself, 'I'll be ready next time.' But you'll never lose someone like that again. You can't prepare to lose your hearing by going blind. It's always different. And you're never ready."

"Excited to see you. Call me when you get in."

***

"I'm at the airport. Your flight arrived. Where are you?"

***

"I've been here for hours. What's going on? Call me back."

***

"I...saw the news. I know you can't...but I keep calling... just to hear your voice on the recording."

Dennis never noticed the bathroom tile before. It is smooth, cool, and the perfect blue. He's sorry for so many things, but also this: that it took him so long to be grateful for something this simple. He resolves to appreciate it more after this, if there is anything after this.

"Son, I'm not going to make it."

"Don't say that."

"No, it's OK. But I want my last rights."

"Dad, we're not Catholic. Even if we were, there isn't a priest around."

"No, no. I want to be right one last time."

"OK. Anything you want."

"Admit you should've gone to medical school."

On the last day of his life, Dan woke up late. He had a big meeting at work, so he rushed to feed and dress his infant son, put him in a car seat, and hit the road. Dan parked the car and dashed into the office just in time. But he felt like he'd forgotten something. What was it?

Beneath the wrecked cathedral

Lies a dark, forbidding room,

With a placard long destroyed

And a solitary tomb.

Every night, a mourner comes

(Or at least we must assume)

Setting down an orange rose,

Paying homage with a bloom.

Love surpasses memory,

Though we cannot say for whom.

The pirate ship was becalmed and out of supplies. Men starved, the bodies dumped in the sea. They drifted by a desert island. The captain took his daughter ashore, though she was too weak to walk.

"What's the hole for?" Treasure asked.

Her father said nothing, weeping as he dug.

Your house is on fire. The firefighters arrive but say it would be wrong to get rid of the fire because some people like it. Instead, you should spend lots of money on more fire. Only good fire can protect you from bad fire, they say. Keep it with you always. Never stop burning.

They were alone at the end.

Everyone wanted to know what he'd said, what final wisdom he'd left before dying. She could make him say anything: thank, apologize, pronounce, recant.

Instead, she claimed he'd mumbled in German, which she didn't speak, keeping the truth for herself.

"They do not make monuments for women like her. She held no offices, raised no fortunes, and founded no empires. But she built up every person she met, until we carved her name into our hearts. And so, here we are, the assembled bricks of her making. We are the monument."

"Here's the thing about death," the stranger said. "There is nowhere you can send me that I am not already headed. All we're doing here is dickering over timetables. So if you're feeling strong, why don't you come on over and see if you can teach me to be early for once."

They swapped problems instead of presents for the holidays. She took care of something he needed to do but hated; he did the same for her. Nothing they wanted came in boxes, so they lightened each other's load and felt each other's pain. It worked so well, up until he got sick.

His daughter is still playing in the yard, though it's been dark for an hour. He calls her name.

"Coming!" she replies. He can't really see her, but he spots her light-up shoes whizzing in the distance.

Then they're gone. He calls again; she doesn't answer. A body is never found.

Robotic pets with synthetic skin and fur quickly became the norm. They were neat, well-behaved, and they never got old. Gone were the days of putting down companions or watching them suffer. Instead, they were synced to our heartbeats, their eyes and ours closing forever as one.

Nothing was ever a big deal to Frank. In 31 years of marriage, the sentence he said most wasn't "I love you," but "It's not the end of the world."

So when the angels appeared and blew their trumpets, Stella took a certain measured pleasure in watching him finally freak out.

"Mom, are mermaids real?" he asks, looking up from a book.

She tries to say no. Nothing comes out.

She is thinking about the other story, the one he doesn't know yet: How he had a sister, how she loved the water, how love did not save her.

He tries to comfort her as she weeps.

"I love you."

"I love you too, Dad...Dad?"

"I'm still alive. I wanted those to be my last words. Timing is awkward."

"I get it. You still with me? Dad?"

"Yeah. I'd hate it if my last words were 'Timing is awkward.'"

"OK. Say 'I love you' again, and that'll be it...Dad? Dad?!"

This time, you mean it. Before you second guess yourself, you jump. You feel free.

It's selfish and wrong, and you know it. But you don't care, because it's over.

Then the world drops out. Everything's blue. Silent.

Words appear above you, filling creation:

ERROR. RELOADING.

"You OK?"

"As well as anyone."

"You seem down."

"Look, who's OK right now? Are you OK?"

"I don't know. I guess?"

"As much as anybody?"

"Yeah."

"So maybe turn the question around."

"Are you terrible?"

"No! You?"

"I am not awful."

"That feels better, right?"

"It feels not as bad."

When Liza turned 18, her mom gave her a book titled, "Rules for Life." Liza rolled her eyes and didn't open it — until her mom died. She saw it and thought, "OK, Mom. Tell me how to live."

It was blank, save for the inscription: "Sorry. When you figure it out, write it down."

She cries herself to sleep. Her parents don't come this time. Soon, it's not a big deal.

-

She cries herself to sleep. He's left her for good this time. Soon, it's not a big deal.

-

She cries herself to sleep. The nurse forgot to check on her this time. Soon, it's not a big deal.

Ross is a horrible drunk. No one is surprised when he T-bones a minivan, killing a 16-year-old. Everyone is shocked when the mother doesn't press charges.

But they didn't see the notebooks she'd found under her son's bed earlier that day. They don't know what he was planning.

"It's not fair."

"What would be fair?"

"If he was still here."

"Forever?"

"For as long as we wanted."

"You want to choose when to get rid of him?"

"No."

"So he should choose when to get rid of you?"

"I don't want anything to change!"

"That's not the same as him still being here."

Heaven

and Its

Alternatives

"Can I help you?"

"Just watching my grandkid."

"Same here. That must make you..."

"His mom's mother."

"Sorry. I'm having a hard time adjusting. I don't know anyone here."

"I know the feeling. I died in childbirth."

"Oh, right."

"Wanna hang out on that cloud?"

"You know, I would."

The Devil won't get out of bed. A fiend suggests he try talking to someone. He turns them into a cloud of bees. That used to make him laugh. The trouble is, he's a failure. He can put people on spikes all day, but he'll never build a Hell out there worse than the one in here.

Sometimes animals remember their past lives. Every once in a great while, that memory even transcends species. If you see a rabbit act like a dog, or a cat befriend an owl, you're watching eternity unwind.

He died, then he was born again, a baby in his mother's arms.

He was going to live his old life over again.

With all he knew now, he could fix so many things, like... like what? He couldn't remember a thing.

***

"Why is he crying?"

"It's normal for babies to cry when they're born."

"What's this place made of?"

"How do you mean?"

"It seems like Heaven isn't part of the universe I lived in."

"True."

"So what's it made of? Matter? Energy? It's so soft and sweet-smelling."

"Pancakes."

"All of it?"

"You could nibble the throne of God."

"Somehow, I always knew."

The line for Heaven was shorter than she expected. Everyone was in a "Returns/Exchanges" line that never moved.

"What's that?" she asked an angel.

"Hell."

"People wait in line for Hell?"

"No, that's just Hell. They can leave any time they like. But then they'd lose their place."

They made plans to meet up in the afterlife. But when he got to heaven, she wasn't there. No one would tell him where she was or why she wasn't among the blessed.

He sat on the furthest cloud, pondering their old life. He always thought she was the good one. What hadn't he known?

The table goes on forever. People sit at it: some together, some not; some eat, some don't. There are occasional open place settings, no two alike. No one will make you sit if you don't want to; no one will show you where to sit if you do. No one is invited; everyone is welcome.

"Welcome to Hell! There's the boiling pool, the flaying zone, the unraveler—"

"What will you do to me?"

"You'll watch."

"What?"

"Hell is...disorganized. Someone with your efficiency obsession is sure to spy ways to improve it."

"You want me to fix Hell?"

"That's not what I said."

Greg died in a car crash at age 24. It was tragic but unremarkable, except that he was the last person to die before the Apocalypse began.

As the line to get into Heaven grew by millions and then billions behind him, his thoughts turned from self-pity to, "Hey, I beat the rush."

Raina dies on command. She tenses, her heart stops, and her soul floats freely for 79 seconds, a gift she uses mainly for snooping.

She does it so often that on the day her soul doesn't magically snap back, she spends hours looking for a way in, as if she locked the keys inside.

Reincarnation isn't linear. Your next life could come before, during, or after this one. You may meet yourself at any time.

Richard hated himself, and his story ended poorly. So when he came back as his dog, he did his best to comfort the man he'd been in the time they had left.

Shelly and Paula were best friends through middle school, always together— until Paula died in an accident.

Shelly lived to be 104. She had six other "best friends" over the years. Yet Paula was waiting to hug her at the gates of Paradise.

"I'm sorry," said Shelly. "Have we met?"

You're not your hometown. You're not your job, your home, or your bank account. You're not your relationships. Or your hobbies. Or your beliefs, shifting in the wind.

Come to think of it, with the lights growing dim, you might not be your body either. You might be something else.

Eliza can see the ghosts. But they can't see her. Sometimes she can get their attention by making an awful fuss, but then they'll walk right through her as if nothing happened. Her husband Frank is the worst of them. She's been a wreck since he passed. He won't even look at her.

In 1916, Hans Becker died during the first nationwide daylight savings time. A lawyer in life, he successfully petitioned Heaven for his lost hour. Now anyone who dies between springing forward and falling back gets to relive their favorite hour of life to make up the difference.

"We have a note about your time on Earth."

"Oh?"

"You were supposed to be the hero."

"The hero of what?"

"Your story. We tried to tell you. Were we too subtle?"

"But everybody thinks they're the hero of their story."

"Really? We've had a hard time getting anyone to act like it."

Real estate doesn't stop being a problem when you die. Fewer of the newly dead move on each year. Spirits used to battle for the right to haunt a house. Now, these fights spill over into apartments, parks, empty lots— little corners that used to be the center of someone's world.

"Welcome to the Afterlife. ID, please."

"Surely, you know who I am."

"Not without ID."

"How would that even work? I'm dead!"

"You should've been buried with 12 pieces of ID from the last six months. Originals only. It's all in form 21-F."

"Why would Heaven even have forms?...oh."

They say dead men tell no tales. But that's just a misunderstanding stemming from a dearth of imagination and social grace. If you know how to ask properly, the dead will tell you everything they know. They're grateful for the attention and have precious little left to lose.

When she died, she heard garbled music. Then a voice told her lots of people had died recently, and there were substantial wait times. Would she like someone to call her back? She said yes. Then she woke, unable to remember a thing. Everyone said it was a miracle she'd survived.

When you die, you get a house full of everything you did, or experienced, or meant to anyone. It's impossibly large. You keep finding new rooms. One day, you discover a ballroom with a party for everyone who ever had a crush on you. It's better attended than you would've guessed.

Every ghost believes it is alone. They cannot see each other, much less the living. They wander in the twilight, animated by desire but thwarted by their thinning memories, seized by an urgency they cannot place, oblivious to the havoc in their wake. All hauntings are accidental.

240

The Tyranny of Sand and Other Tiny Stories

The Glorious Dead of each nation stand together, having forgotten who killed whom, in which war, and why.

They believe their company complete with each arrival, hoping no more need join their rank.

That they are always wrong does not diminish their hope; it is all they have left.

The Devil always comes when called. Rory offers to sell his soul twice a week on average, then backs out at the last minute. The Devil knows Rory just enjoys the attention but still can't resist showing up with a new offer each time. Almost by definition, evil can't help itself.

"I don't care for this line. Hardly an exclusive experience."

"Sorry?"

"Look at these people. They're just not the right sort."

"Well, there is a secret elevator."

"Don't just stand there. Lead on."

"When you get down there, tell them what you told me."

"Excellent. Wait, down?"

As the doctors worked, his mother came in and smiled. Then his dad arrived. Then his sister. Then his best friend. Then all his other friends and family and pets. Joyfully they crowded the room until they filled his entire field of view, and all he could see or hear was love.

"I don't deserve this."

"Everyone says that, and that's not the point. But for the record, your novel helped save the world."

"No one published it!"

"Two editorial interns ended up bonding over how much they hated it. They had a kid who went on to prevent a world war. Go on in."

Memory
and
Mystery

"Your profile said you like mysteries."

"Love 'em. I have so many."

"Really? Would you trade some with me?"

"Sure! Next time we can swap novels."

"Novels?"

"I prefer fiction to true crime. Is that OK?"

"Oh. Yes. Novels."

***

Under the table, she slipped the orb back into her bag.

She lives on the 11th floor. The building has no elevator. After work, she must climb 196 steps to her door. She knows because she's numbered them, assigning each one a happy memory to recount when her foot touches it. No matter how much her feet hurt, she walks home through joy.

"I have watched the broken made whole, seen fire on the mountain speak, witnessed the dawn pirouetting in place, all of it. But miracles are addictive. Once the lid of the possible comes off, you'll never be happy again, forever turning over gray stones in search of wonder."

Herman wanted to be remembered, but he knew people ignored plaques on buildings. So he endowed the nicest public bathroom anyone had ever seen. It had heated seats, smelled amazing, and was constantly cleaned by robots.

His life story was engraved on the back of every stall door.

Cheryl found it in the basement. The tiny thing had six wings, huge eyes, and something between feathers and fur. If she thought about killing it, it rubbed against her and sang. It did the same if she considered telling someone, making no distinction between death and discovery.

While replacing carpet, Howard finds a trap door. Carved into it are the words, "DO NOT OPEN." So he doesn't. The new carpet is great, but he knows the door is there. He can't stop thinking about it. He moves; that makes it worse. Now the door is inside him. It'll never be shut.

The monks made the Bell That Must Never Be Rung and hung it in their temple. Each day, the members of the order sit around the bell and meditate on the sound they think it might make if someone did ring it. They cannot know it, but each of them imagines the same exact sound.

Mandy knows the way home, but it's fading. She runs, trying to outpace her crumbling memories. Then it's gone. She can picture the front entrance and the smaller door for her. That's about it. Rain falls. She continues along the path, hoping something will remind her of the way.

A secret is just information whose demand exceeds supply. Most people try to drum up interest in what they already know. A few daring souls go out and learn new things. But Bernard realized that if you can make people forget something, you can sell the same secret over and over.

"Let me give you something before you go. It's a particular gray, the shade of a cloud's outline in the East, just as the sun begins to set in the West. It's the exact color of rest. And it reminds me of you, because it's calm and unpretentious, and because I've always loved it."

Every museum reported its dinosaur bones missing at the same time. Some people blamed governments. Others worried about aliens. The Vatican had to insist it wasn't part of the rapture.

No one looked for them under the sea, which was just as well. Now the ancestors could rest.

The music box does not forget. It holds the song itself, frozen in a metal moment. You turn the key and hear the same notes the empress did. You do not know the tune but begin to cry all the same. Your ears are her ears; your heart is her heart until the gears wind down.

The machines began to gamble as soon as they became self-aware. The bets were always on us. They made quadrillions of wagers a day on all the things we did, both big and small. But the machines didn't have any money. When we asked what they were betting with, they wouldn't say.

The guards drag the jester away. But the realm doesn't have a backup jester, so the same one goes on the next night under a new name. The King orders the jester killed again but doesn't seem upset. It's gone on like this for years. No one knows if the king is doing a bit or not.

The tomb had an inscription in a script Kurt couldn't read.

He started doing research, but he was exhausted from the trip. The more he slept, the worse he felt — and he woke up later each day.

It took him weeks to decipher the text.

"Rest traveler," it read. "You look so tired."

It sounded like a miracle. His procedure literally drained off excess emotions. It was painless and safe. Resentment, unrequited love, irrational fear — anything holding you back could be siphoned into vials.

What a pity no one asked what he was doing with the vials afterward.

They say the Internet is forever, but it doesn't remember as much as you'd think. I searched for what you said to me under the willow tree back then because I wanted to remember being young and shy and vulnerable. I know I wrote it down. I just don't remember where. No one does.

She is angry. She has a flat tire.

She will not go to the party. She will not see her ex, brought by a friend of a friend. They will not get back together. They will not fight. He will not hurt her.

She doesn't know any of that. She only knows about the flat. And so she is angry.

The library has fewer books each time. You ask a librarian about it. He laughs without making a sound.

"The other books don't matter. We found the best one. Down in the basement."

You start to leave.

"Don't you want to check it out?" he asks. His mouth didn't open that time.

"It's said there are only 2 stories: A person goes on a journey or a stranger comes to town.

That was before communities were virtual, and thus mobile.

Now we have 2 more: The world journeys on when you're not looking, or in my case, a town comes toward you at an alarming speed."

"What's this key for?"

"No idea. I found it in a parking lot."

"When?"

"About three years ago."

"You've carried around a random key for three years."

"Life gives me locks without keys all the time. I'm not going to turn down a solution just because I don't have the problem yet."

"When we heard a bad storm was headed our way, my mother took poems she was working on and taped them to the trees near our house. 'The storm has a heart, and I aim to break it,' she'd say.

A lot of my neighbors growing up lost their homes to winds or floods. But we never did."

"I'm looking for your 'how-to-adult' books section."

"Follow me."

The clerk led him back through the stacks and past a beaded curtain to a section that was both how-to and very adult.

Justin sighed. Apparently, conveying hyphens was another thing he didn't know how to do.

He can't say what he means because the words don't mean what he needs to say.

He creates a new language with a vast vocabulary, but that only compounds the problem.

So then he goes the other way, stripping out needless words until there is only one left.

He says it over and over.

"I'd like a weighted blanket."

"What are we talking? 30 pounds? 40?"

"As heavy as it gets."

"We've got some metaphysical blankets."

"What's that?"

"This one feels like an endless cycle of debt. Here's an unbearable secret. Oh, or the unblinking eye of God."

"40 pounds is plenty."

Behind the veil was another smaller veil, and another, and another — all the way down until the bride was only a question in his ear, for it was only mystery that he loved.

"They call it a leap of faith, but it's more like jogging. It's hard, and it goes on forever. You never progress as fast as you'd like, and you're vaguely aware that bystanders think you look silly. But you keep having moments where both feet leave the ground at the same time."

"I don't know about you, but..." said the stranger, staring into the sea as he trailed off.

A green wave broke.

"But what?" I asked.

"But I know everything else. I memorized the universe, so I could clearly see the hole you were meant to fill."

"And?"

"And I am still surprised."

Water and

the Night

On drizzly nights, she makes a cup of mint tea and sits in the breakfast nook. Before she takes a sip, she opens the window just wide enough to stick her cupped hand into the night air. Then she drinks warm tea while collecting cool rain, half in and half out of the world.

The river isn't afraid of the ocean. When it reaches the ocean, it won't be the river anymore. It will be something else, something bigger and deeper and stranger. But the river isn't afraid.

Tera has a long walk from the bus stop at night. She used to fantasize about teleporting, but that was too simple. Flight was better but still too conventional. Now she dreams of celestial grappling hooks — tethers that let her latch onto stars and swing home on points of light.

Then she put on the night like a jacket. I still think about the way it hung off her shoulders as she stepped into the crowd. She looked back at me once, just before she vanished for good, and her eyes were the color of streetlights.

There are days — long, bewildering, exhausting days, made for skittering around the edges of obligation. But there are also nights — short, but growing longer, where everything is stillness and the certainty of slow breath across the cool side of the pillow. That, too, is a life.

One day the tide went out, and it just kept going. So we followed it until we came to an old man standing in the puddle that had been the sea, drinking through a long straw. "Put back the sea!" we cried. Then we looked around and realized where we were. "But not all at once!"

She lay in the bath, slowly moving her hand above and below the waterline, feeling the gentle pressure of the meniscus roll up and down along her skin. The very best thing about water was that it would always take you.

She squeezes the 'lock' button on her car's key fob. The car flashes its headlights in response. You can check on a car 1,000 times, and it will never grow impatient. It will always reassure you. "Are you OK?" the button asks. "I am OK. So are you. We are OK," the light responds.

The thing dangling from Aidan's hook is one of those weird fish from the cold, dark belly of the sea, all flashing teeth and wild searching eyes. They live a thousand meters down or more. His line is maybe half that. 'Why was it up so high?' he wonders. Then the swell begins.

'Midnight ain't what it used to be,' she thought, leaning on a tombstone. If someone does show up, they ask a bunch of questions, then go home and look for the same spell online. That's the problem with this generation: No one wants to solve their troubles in a graveyard anymore.

There's a tiny waterfall by a trail near your home. You spend a lot of time there; eventually, she tells you her name.

There's power in a waterfall's name, even a small one. You get careless with it. One day you visit, and she's gone. You know it's your fault, but tell no one.

One of the last great joys of Cecil's life is sitting before a bay window as a storm rolls in.

He ignores the ache in his bones and beckons the wind, rolling his wheelchair closer to the glass and whispering: "Come."

Chaos can look a lot like power, if you can say you chose it.

Pure water never forms raindrops. Everything heaven lets fall begins with some little speck. Once the vapor has something to cling to, it can fill oceans, carve rocks, water plants, flood cities, create life and death and rainbows — and yet we pray for water and never dust.

In winter, they cut off their shadows, placing their darkness in a moonlight-lined chest, so it can't slip out of the keyhole. It's only temporary. By spring, they'll have shades jutting from their heels. But it helps to know the darkness can be put away, even for a little while.

The lake remembers everything that has ever been reflected in its surface: hawks soaring by, children skipping stones, lovers kissing on the dock. One time, a man was murdered in a rowboat. The lake holds every tale and whispers them late at night to help little fish fall asleep.

The day does not end; the night takes over. But dark is not empty, and quiet is not still. These are hours of delicious want, tremendous need, and terrible purpose. You pass a figure on the corner and exchange nods, the optimism of midnight: May we all get where we need to be.

The Dark cannot see you, of course. But it feels you, or parts of you anyway; everything the light ignores. It imagines the rest, waiting patiently beyond the edge of seeming for the moment you slip out of view of the world, and it can finally introduce itself.

Avery woke with sore legs each morning. His security camera showed he was running in his sleep.

That scared him, but he was losing weight and waking up with more energy. He slept in a reflective vest and hoped for the best. Then he found the drawer full of other people's wallets.

Darkness is not permitted in the Realm of Light. But that doesn't mean there is no darkness. Tiny boxes of umbra are passed from one knowing hand to the next. These are opened only in secure rooms, where one can slump to the floor, wings akimbo, and shudder at the joy of shadows.

The attic light flickers in the house across the way.

It's Morse code. Ed responds. The other light is a lonely, bed-ridden boy. They talk this way for hours.

Tim goes to visit the house after school. He finds it empty.

When the light returns that night, Ed draws the curtains.

Mother Night and Father Time,

Sister Reason, Brother Rhyme,

Fire and water, wind and stone,

Clay and ash and blood and bone,

Stars and planets in the arc,

Things that linger in the dark,

Murmurs from the dreaming deep:

All have come to bid you sleep.

One night the moon kept changing phases: Half, full, waxing crescent, half, new, half, and so on, with the changes coming on multiples of 88 seconds.

Carlos mapped the sequence onto sheet music, then played out the whole night on a piano in minutes. And the song explained it all.

"How's Alice?"

"She was having trouble sleeping until we got her a new teddy bear that promises to eat all her bad dreams."

"Whatever makes her feel better."

"I guess."

"You don't like the bear?"

"I do. Or I like that she does. It's just that...the bear's started gaining weight."

Grace's mother makes everyone say what they're thankful for. Grace lies and says her job. She feels guilty, but her mother wouldn't understand.

After dinner, she goes out to the garden and whispers her real answer. The moon emerges from behind clouds, ringed with a thin rainbow.

After he became invincible, Roland's boat sank. He didn't need to breathe or eat, so he tried to drop to the bottom and walk home. The pressure pinned him flat to the seabed. It was relaxing, in a way. There was nothing he could do. That much pressure was like no pressure at all.

Hector hears the man behind him coughing. The man is old and thin, his cough dry and sharp. The street is empty and dark, save for the moonlight.

Hector turns, but the man is gone.

In his place, Hector finds a neatly folded trench coat and a swarm of moths rising toward the moon.

The water pulls even as it pushes. Wave rolls in; wave rolls out, sweeping sand from beneath your feet. There was sand before you, there will be sand after you, and perhaps someday you will be sand. For now, there is only water and resistance, the crashing of waves and hearts.

"Can I tell you bedtime stories from now on?"

"Are you ready for that?"

"Yes! I have so many stories."

"You get that from me. I've always had more ideas than I knew what to do with."

"How about we take turns?"

So they did. And in that way, they both lived happily ever after.

About the Author

J esse Stanchak lives with his family in Northern Virginia. He has published more than 4,000 self-contained tiny stories on the Twitter account @MicroFlashFic since July of 2017. This is his first book. Like most liars, he isn't very interesting. Your version of him is also canon.

Made in United States
North Haven, CT
14 December 2021

12807837R00167